*For Robin   J.G.*
*For Richard Harris, 30 March 2006   T.M.*

Library of Congress Cataloging-in-Publication Data

Goodwin, John.
   An arkful of animal stories / John Goodwin ; illustrated by Tina Macnaughton. —
1st North American ed.
      p. cm.
   Summary: From the lofty giraffe to the tiny mouse, the animals aboard Noah's ark
use their God-given talents to help each other endure their lengthy stay indoors.
   ISBN 0-8198-0782-6 (hardcover)
   [1. Animals—Fiction. 2. Noah's ark—Fiction. 3. Deluge—Fiction.]
I. Macnaughton, Tina, ill. II. Title.
PZ7.G6257Ar 2008
[E]—dc22
                                    2007043075
Text copyright © 2006, John Goodwin

Illustrations copyright © 2006, Tina Macnaughton

Original edition published in English under the title *An Arkful of Animal Stories* by
Lion Hudson plc, Oxford, England

Edition copyright © 2006, Lion Hudson plc

The moral rights of the author and illustrator have been asserted.

"P" and PAULINE are registered trademarks of the Daughters of St. Paul.

First North American edition

Published by Pauline Books & Media, 50 Saint Pauls Avenue, Boston, MA
02130-3491. www.pauline.org.

Printed in China.

Pauline Books & Media is the publishing house of the Daughters of St. Paul,
 an international congregation of women religious serving the Church with the
communications media.

For the location of the Pauline Books & Media Centers nearest you, visit
www.pauline.org.

1 2 3 4 5 6 7 8 9                                          11 10 09 08

# An ARKFUL of ANIMAL stories

John Goodwin
Illustrated by Tina Macnaughton

Pauline
BOOKS & MEDIA
Boston

# Contents

# Noah

When Noah heard God call to him, he was frightened.

"Don't be scared, Noah," said God in a friendly voice. "I've heard that you're a shipbuilder—is that true?"

"It is true," answered Noah.

"Excellent," said God. "I want you to build the greatest ship in the world. This ark will have to be big enough to hold two of every animal that breathes. Use all your skill, Noah, and ask all your family to help you. When the earth begins to flood, you and the animals must board the ark. Your lives will depend on it."

# The Hippos

Splish. Splash. Splash!
The rain was falling fast.
It hadn't stopped for three
whole days and nights.
Hundreds of animals still
needed to board the ark.
Out of the jungle they
cantered. Over land they
scampered. In the air
they flew. Chattering,
squawking,
trumpeting! Monkeys
had tied creepers to
the ark, so crawly
animals could climb
along them up into safety
without getting their feet
wet.
But time was running out.
Already the ark was floating, and
the land was disappearing under the water.

"Help!" cried the animals left on land. "It's too far for us to jump onto the ark. What can we do?"

Then they saw two hippos wallowing in the mud, having one last bath. They lifted their huge snouts and turned to look at the frightened animals. Lumbering forward, they held their bodies still in the water to make two giant stepping stones between the dry land and the ark.

"But I'm too scared," whispered the armadillo.

One of the hippos lifted his head to give a friendly wink. Then they both began to snuffle with a gentle, muddy sort of sound.

The lions raised their heads and stepped forward onto the first stepping stone.

The hippo's back was perfectly still and steady. With another step, the lions reached the second hippo, and with a third they stepped safely into the ark.

"It's our turn now," whispered the camel.

Two by two the animals on the land followed and carefully stepped from hippo to hippo into the ark.

"Thank you, God," sang the hippos in full-throated harmony. "You have kept us calm in a time of crisis."

# The Giraffe

The giraffe's neck was amazingly long. It reached right up to the roof of the ark. But it didn't stop there. Oh, no. It went through a round window and high into the air.

The giraffe didn't see the rest of the animals trying to sleep in the ark below her. Instead, her lips quivered and her teeth chomped. She wound her neck cleverly to reach the very highest leaves on the last unflooded trees. Chomp, chomp, chomp.

Way down below her, a tiny animal squeaked.

"What are you doing up there?" asked the mouse in her loudest voice.

"Eating," said the giraffe between mouthfuls.

"What else are you doing?" squeaked the mouse.

"Looking," said the giraffe, not used to making conversation.

"What does it look like up there?" squeaked the mouse.

"There's water everywhere," said the giraffe, trying to be chattier.

"How deep is it?" squeaked the mouse.

"Deep enough to flood most of the earth. Soon it will cover even the tall mountains," said the giraffe, who had never done so much talking.

"I wish I could see that," said the mouse in a very sad squeak, trying to stand on tiny tiptoes.

The giraffe stopped chomping and lowered her neck into the ark.

"Climb up onto my neck, little one," she said, "and I'll show you."

The mouse had never been so high nor seen so far.

She talked so much about her adventure that very soon lots of the other smaller animals, one by one, came to take a ride on the giraffe's neck.

"Thank you, God," said the giraffe, "for all the new friends I've made. We all need to be friends for the adventure ahead."

# The Elephant

In the ark, the animals were all busy. They were brushing and sweeping. They were scrubbing and cleaning and polishing. Everyone was helping, except the elephant. He was doing nothing at all.

Hour after hour he sat lazily on his own with his eyes half closed.

The animals were working all through the day. They were sifting and sorting. They were mending and fixing and carrying and shifting. But the elephant was still doing nothing at all. He sat idly on the straw.

The turtle was tired and the skunk was shattered. The zebra was zapped and the wombat was whacked. Even the millipede was listless and the flea was fatigued.

"Oh dear," they all groaned. "Our brains are boggled and our bodies bedraggled."

"The elephant's done nothing," grumbled the gorilla.

"Lift your trunk, will you?" barked the seal.

But the elephant didn't move a single muscle.

Then night fell. The animals expected to fall asleep at once, but somehow they still felt busy inside.

"I'm thinking of home," buzzed the bee.

"Me, too," mooed the cow.

That's when the elephant moved his trunk.

"Listen to my story," he said. "I've been writing it in my head all day.

"When the sun rises in the jungle, it is the brightest and most beautiful thing in the world," began the elephant. "Trees shimmer and all things glow in the greenness…"

His story carried the animals into the world of their dreams. The quiet words were soothing to their ears. Soon they were all fast asleep.

An elephant never forgets anything. God gave him a special gift as a storyteller, just as God gave every creature their own special talent.

# The Lion

The blackness of the sky was lit up in a fierce storm as lightning flashed and thunder crashed. The rain poured down in buckets, and everything was awash with water.

In a far corner of the ark, the lion had his paws over his eyes. A tiny flea usually liked to hide deep in the lion's mane, but at that moment she hopped out onto the tip of the lion's nose.

"Excuse me, mighty one," whispered the flea.

"What is it?" replied the lion grumpily.

"Why do you have your paws over your eyes?" asked the flea.

"I'm trying to think," said the lion.

"Are you scared of the lightning?" asked the flea.

"Oh, no," said the lion. "I love lightning."

Just then, a huge clap of thunder boomed in the heavens, and the lion moved his paws to his ears.

The lion pretended he hadn't heard the question, so the flea hopped closer to his ear.

"Are you afraid of the thunder?" asked the flea.

16

"Oh, no," said the lion. "I can roar more loudly than any thunder."

At that moment, the ark was hit by a huge wave. It rocked and rolled and pitched and tossed. The lion started to tremble.

"Before you ask, little flea," said the lion, "I'm shivering because I'm cold."

The flea looked into the lion's eye. She didn't believe the lion was telling the truth.

Neither did the rabbit nor the gazelle nor any of the animals that had gathered around.

The lion slowly lowered his paw and looked at them all.

"Oh, dear," he said. "I'm supposed to be king of all animals. Wasn't I first to step onto the ark? Yet now, I admit, I'm very afraid."

"We all are," said the flea. "It's always best to tell the truth. Then we can help one another."

# The Rattlesnake

Below deck it was very crowded. The ark was big, but fitting in all the hundreds and hundreds of different animals was still a bit of a squash.

One night the rattlesnake found himself

squished between the bison's bottom and an ape's armpit.

"This is seriously sniffy. I can't squirm or shake or slide or slither. I can't even sleep. And what's even worse is that I can't rattle at all. What good is a rattlesnake without a rattle?" he sighed. "It's like having a camel without a hump or an elephant without a trunk."

The rattlesnake slipped into a sulk. In the desert, all the animals used to marvel at the way he rolled his Rs. "RRRRRRRR!"

"I haven't even rolled my Rs since I've been on this stinky ship," he sighed. "I need room to rattle my body and roll my Rs. They go together. Like slide and slither."

After another sleepless night, the rattlesnake was silently seething. Then, as the sun began to light the sky, the rooster sang his morning song.

"COCK-A-DOODLE-DOO!"

The cricket clicked his heels, the hyena laughed, the swan hissed, and the duck quacked.

"QUACK QUACK QUACK!"

"Such a surprise," said the rattlesnake to himself.

"If there's room for them, then there's room for me."

He made a tiny slither and tried to rattle. There was no sound at all.

The ape yawned and grunted and scratched herself. She made just enough room for a reasonable wriggle. The wriggle rose to a rattle as a roll of Rs rang out.

"RRRRRRR!"

The rattlesnake rejoiced as he rattled again.

It was a thank-you rattle for the bright new day dawning.

# The Monkeys

No onions. No turnips. And no carrots.

"But I love carrots," neighed the horse. "My belly will ache if I don't have carrots to munch."

"My belly has been aching all day," whined the weasel. "There was nothing for me to eat at breakfast."

"Me neither," moaned the hedgehog in a particularly prickly voice.

Only the owl had any wise words to say.

"Food is scarce. We must all share and save."

"Share and save. Share and save." The sheep bleated the words over and over again.

Late in the evening, the elephant finished telling one of his stories and let out a very loud trumpet. All the animals came running, crawling, and skipping to a big wooden table in the center of the ark. A huge cloth covered the table.

The sheep bleated, "It's bananas, bananas. We can smell bananas."

The elephant whipped away the cloth with a flick of his trunk.

To everyone's amazement, there were no

bananas on the table,
only piles of brown banana skins.

"Somebody's stolen the bananas. Who can
it be?" growled the tiger.

The kangaroo had to empty her pouch.

The eagle was sent to check the jackdaw's nest.

Everyone searched the whole ark, but no one
found a single banana.

All this time the two monkeys had been
under the suspicious eye of the donkey. She
noticed that their cheeks were bulging.

"Have you eaten the bananas?" she asked them.

Both monkeys shook their heads slowly.

The owl flew up for a closer look.

"Their cheeks must be stuffed with bananas,"
he hooted.

The monkeys looked at one another. They
scratched their heads. They huddled close
together and tried to swallow hard.

"Ooh, we've been found out," they gibbered.

The elephant came and poked each of them
with his trunk.

"You can't have eaten them all," he said.
"Where are all the others?"

"On the roo-oo-oof," sobbed the monkeys.

"Horumph," said the elephant. "In that case,
you must go and fetch them back."

The monkeys were glad to!

# The Glowworms

One night, in the deepest room in the ark, it was pitch black. It was so dark you couldn't see a flipper in front of your face or an elephant before your eyes. You couldn't see tails or claws or paws or beaks. Even the cat and the tiger, whose eyes were used to seeing in the night, could hardly see anything but shapes and shadows.

In a little knothole in the timber, two glow-worms began to whisper together.

"Time for us to show ourselves," they murmured.

"Where shall we go to?" they whispered.

"I'll crawl up onto the rafters," said Mrs. Glowworm. "You can fly up there first."

"No, no," said Mr. Glowworm, "I'll crawl up with you."

"But it's so high," said Mrs. Glowworm. "It'll take us ages to crawl."

"All the more reason to go together," replied Mr. Glowworm.

Off they went together. Inch by inch they crawled, over the knots and splinters in the wooden planking. They climbed higher and higher until at last they found themselves on the very top rafter.

"Take a moment to catch your breath," said Mr. Glowworm. "Then… GLOW!"

A few seconds later Mrs. Glowworm began to glow magnificently in the dark.

"It's a miracle," murmured the marmot.

"Is it a star, high in the sky?" stammered the starfish.

"It's the North Star," said the polar bear confidently.

"If only it were the moon," howled the wolf longingly.

As Mrs. Glowworm went on glowing, the animals began to talk of the time when the flood would be over. Then they could leave the ark and live, not under a roof, but under the sun and the moon and the stars.

The glowworms had given the animals hope in their darkest hour.

# The Hare

The animals were fed up. They had been on the ark for days upon days upon days, and still it hadn't stopped raining. The yak yawned and the sloth slumbered. The bat was bored and the donkey was drowsy.

"Are we nearly there yet?" squeaked the mouse.

No one answered.

"We must be nearly there," squeaked the mouse. But her words fell into another long silence.

The mouse broke the silence again.

"Surely we're nearly there?" she squeaked.

"Hush, you annoying creature," snapped the alligator, showing his teeth.

"Keep your squeaks to yourself, mouse," clucked the duck.

"Don't cluck, duck," roared the tiger.

"Don't roar, tiger," howled the wolf. "You're giving me a terrible headache."

The argument went on and on. The duck clucked at the tiger, the tiger roared at the wolf.

The wolf howled for want of something to do, and soon the dog and the fox and the jackal joined in. The fuss lasted all day long, and every animal was so sad.

The hare felt cross at all this nonsense. She tapped her foot…and then remembered her favorite thumping rhythm.

"Thump thump thump, thump thump thump."

Soon the rattlesnake joined in. "Rattle rattle rattle, rattle rattle rattle."

"Hum hum hum, hum hum hum," buzzed the bee.

"Caw caw caw, caw caw caw," called the crow.

The animal band was growing. Soon the orangutan drummed his chest, the elephant trumpeted, the hyena laughed, and the bison bashed her feet. An animal orchestra was in full swing!

That's when the hare began to dance. She leaped and ran and jumped and capered. It was a skippereen sort of dance that everyone wanted to join.

Soon the sheep were shimmying, the
kangaroos were kicking, and the porcupines
were pirouetting. Then the whole ark began
to rock!

# The Raven

"Listen," cawed the raven.

"I can't hear anything," purred the cat, quietly licking her paws.

"Exactly," cawed the raven. "You can't hear anything."

"I can't be figuring out your raven riddles," purred the cat, preening her whiskers and flicking her tail.

"Hearing nothing means it's stopped raining!" cawed the raven loudly.

The animals peered out the porthole windows. Someone drew back a latch and opened the hatch. Paws and toes climbed up steps. Heads and bodies, tails and toes appeared on deck. It was true. The rain had stopped.

"Hooray!" cried the parrot.

"Hurrah!" shouted the monkey.

"Hallelujah!" sang one and all.

Three days went by. There was no more rain.

The flood water began to drop. The ark crunched against something solid: land at last.

"Raven," called Noah. "I want you here."

"You are the clever one, Raven," said Noah, holding the bird on the back of his hand. "Seek out the craggy mountain tops. When you return we'll know you have found dry land."

The bird's jet-black body soared into the sky, but a strong wind blew him sideways. On he flew, struggling hard.

"Of course I'll find land, of course I'll find land," he cawed.

But even though he flew and flew, he saw nothing but brown flood water. His body was tired, and his heart was heavy.

Then at last the raven saw a small cluster of rocks rising out of the water.

"They will make a perfect nesting site," he cawed as he flew down to them.

He rested a while on the rocks and gathered his strength. He pecked at tiny green shoots growing out of a crevice in the rock.

"Soon other birds will leave the ark," he cawed. "Soon my mate will come to join me."

Time passed, and the raven grew lonely. No other birds came to join him. But still he cawed and waited and cawed again, trusting that he would not be alone for ever.

# The Dove

There was sadness on the ark. Long days passed, and the raven didn't return. Still, everyone scanned the skies and the silvery surface of the sea for any sign of the returning bird. But it was all for nothing.

Every crumb of food had been eaten. Every animal was feeling low. Something had to be done. But what?

Noah looked around carefully at all the birds perched in the rafters. "Another bird will have to do what the raven could not," he said.

Should he choose the flamingo to fly off next, or would it be the golden eagle that took to the skies? What about the swift or the swallow, the gull or the heron?

Noah chose the dove. He whispered a prayer and set her free. Every animal prayed for her safe return.

Time plodded by. Still the skies were empty.

"If the raven failed, what chance has the dove?" whispered the sloth. "She's rather plump for such a long journey."

The hawk fixed his beady eye on the horizon. Suddenly he flapped his wings and screeched out loud.

"What can you see? What have you spotted?" everyone squealed.

"A tiny dot high in the sky!" cried the hawk.

As the dot grew into a small winged shape, a huge double rainbow formed in the heavens.

It spanned the sky in glorious brilliant color.
Each band was a dazzle. Under its arch, the dove
returned with an olive twig in her beak.

"Look," said Noah. "God has given us a
signal of peace in the new world that
is about to begin. Let us give
thanks for his almighty
blessing!"